Emily Gravett
BEAR & HARE
Snow!

Simon & Schuster Books for Young Readers

New York London Toronto Sydney New Delhi

One morning Bear and Hare
went outside and saw . . .

OW!

Hare loves snow.

Bear and Hare caught snowflakes
on their tongues.

They made snow prints,

and snow angels.

Snow hares,

and snow bears.

Bear rolled a big snowball,

and Hare rolled a little snowball.

LOTS of little snowballs!

Then Bear and Hare went . . .

Home?

SLEDDING!

Hare and Bear LOVE snow!

For Fin

SIMON & SCHUSTER BOOKS FOR YOUNG READERS

An imprint of Simon & Schuster Children's Publishing Division

1230 Avenue of the Americas, New York, New York 10020

Copyright © 2014 by Emily Gravett

Originally published in 2014 in Great Britain by Macmillan Children's Books

Published by arrangement with Macmillan Publishers Limited • First US edition 2015

All rights reserved, including the right of reproduction in whole or in part in any form.

SIMON & SCHUSTER BOOKS FOR YOUNG READERS is a trademark of Simon & Schuster, Inc.

For information about special discounts for bulk purchases, please contact Simon &

Schuster Special Sales at 1·866·506·1949 or business@simonandschuster.com.

The Simon & Schuster Speakers Bureau can bring authors to your live event. For more

information or to book an event, contact the Simon & Schuster Speakers Bureau at 1·866·248·3049

or visit our website at www.simonspeakers.com.

The text for this book is set in Pastonchi.

The illustrations for this book are rendered in pencil, watercolor, and wax crayons.

Manufactured in China • 0715 MCM • 10 9 8 7 6 5 4 3 2 1

Library of Congress Cataloging·in·Publication Data

Gravett, Emily, author, illustrator.

Bear and Hare snow! / Emily Gravett.

pages cm.—(Bear and Hare)

Originally published in the United Kingdom by

Macmillan Children's Books, 2014.

Summary: Friends Bear and Hare go out and play in the snow.

ISBN 978·1·4814·4514·6 (hardcover)

ISBN 978·1·4814·4515·3 (eBook)

[1. Snow—Fiction. 2. Friendship—Fiction.

3. Bears—Fiction. 4. Hares—Fiction.]

I. Title.

PZ7.G77577Bg 2015

[E]—dc23

2014038510